Merry lumping
Christmas to:

From:

PRICE STERN SLOAN
Published by the Penguin Group
Penguin Group (USA) LLC, 375 Hudson Street, New York, New York 10014, USA

USA | Canada | UK | Ireland | Australia | New Zealand | India | South Africa | China

penguin.com
A Penguin Random House Company

Published in 2014 by Price Stern Sloan, a division of Penguin Young Readers Group, 345 Hudson Street, New York, New York 10014. *PSS!* is a registered trademark of Penguin Group (USA) LLC. Manufactured in China.

Slamacowtastic design by Giuseppe Castellano
Mathematical art created digitally

ISBN 978-0-8431-8068-8 · 10 9 8 7 6 5 4 3 2 1

A CHRISTMAS-TASTIC CAROL

by
Max Brallier
illustrated by
Emily Warren

Price Stern Sloan
An Imprint of Penguin Group (USA), LLC

Christmas Eve . . .

Ice King stood at the window of his castle.
"I HATE Christmas," he cried out. "What a miserable hassle!
People celebrating, dancing and stuff!
To them all I say, *Bah! Hum butt!!!*"

Gunters at his feet, dressed in Christmas gear,
were waiting to go out and spread Christmas cheer.
"So, you penguin fools wish to celebrate?
I say *NO*! My heart is full of Christmas *hate*!"

With that, Ice King climbed into his icy-cold bed,
and laid down his angry, icy-cold head.
He was snuggled up in his icy-cold robes,
and after a time, his eyes began to close.

Ice King planned to sleep until Christmas was done.
He had no interest in wintry fun.
But something was coming that he did not expect.
Something quite ghoulish approached as he slept.

"What the junk?" the Ice King howled. "Who are you?"
But as the figure flew closer, old Ice King knew . . .
"Marceline!" he shrieked. "Why are you here?"
But Marceline was quiet as she slowly drew near.

"This night," she whispered, "I go by a different name."
"What do you mean?" Ice King snapped. "Have you gone insane?"
She moved from the shadows, and he let out a gasp,
as Marceline howled, *"I am the Ghost of Christmas Past!"*

Ice King shrieked, "Please, I don't understand . . ."
"Then come," she said, "let us fly, old man!"
Off in the distance, they heard Christmas bells chime.
Everything changed, as they moved through space and time . . .

Suddenly, somehow, they were viewing a scene.
But they weren't really *there*—it was more like a dream.

Ice King's eyes went wide, and he was like, "Whoa!"
He saw *himself* from many, *many* years ago . . .
"I don't understand. What the junk is the deal?"
Marceline replied, "It's the past, dude. None of it's real!"

"Who's that?" Ice King asked. "Some kind of princess?"
"That's Betty!" she said. "Your love, celebrating Christmas."
"Tell me more," Ice King pleaded. "She seems kind of rad."
"She was your fiancée," Marceline replied. "Until you went mad."

Marceline beckoned. "C'mon, there's more."
And they moved to a time after the war . . .

Arriving, he heard the sounds of laughter and cheer.
He recognized the scene as they slowly moved near.

"It's us!" Ice King exclaimed as he pointed below
at young Marcy and Ice King, playing in the snow.
"Our rinky-dink Christmas, nothing was greater!"
But then Ice King remembered all that happened later . . .

"Christmas was ruined when I lost control of my brain!
I hate this holiday, it's *lame, lame, lame!*"
Ice King howled, "Take me home now, you ghoul!"
Marceline frowned at her friend, the confused old fool . . .

And then, in a flash, Ice King was back in his home.
Marceline was gone—and he was alone.
"It was a dream!" Ice King said. "Or worse, a nightmare!"
But when he looked to the door, he felt a stir in the air.

Ice King gulped—for he knew this night was not through.
He slid out of the bed to get a better view.
Whilst he tiptoed across the icy-cold floor,
his heart pounded as he reached for the door.

He flung it open and into the room he went . . .

Ice King groaned. "No you're not, you're LSP!"
"Not tonight," she said. *"Tonight I'm not me!"*

LSP grabbed Ice King by his bony old wrists
and said, "C'mon, Ice Jerk, we're taking a trip!"
"But how?" he asked. "I'm not a ghost, you fool!"
LSP sighed. "If I'm a ghost, you're a ghost—it's, like, ghost rules!"

There was a burst of color, and soon they were standing in the Candy Kingdom, with Candy People dancing!

There was Princess Bubblegum, handing out toys, and gazing upon her kingdom with holiday joy. And trumpets were playing, and bells were ringing. Candy People playing and laughing and singing.

There was a thawing, then, of the king's icy-cool heart.
"I want to join in the fun!" he said. "I want to take part!"
But LSP said, "No, Ice King, you're coming with me.
There is much more that you need to see . . ."

The kingdom fell away, and the people departed.
And then from the grass, something strange started.
From the dirt rose a tree of a very odd sort.
Ice King realized, "Hey, it's Finn and Jake's Tree Fort!"

Ice King held the hand of his lumpy ghost guide
as they floated up to the window and peered inside.
There they saw BMO, in the corner, looking ill.
Sweating one second, the next second a chill.

Poor little BMO had the robot flu!
Ice King hoped there was something he could do.

"Stop this, ghost! Let me save BMO's poor soul!
With my icy magic, I can make BMO whole!"
But LSP grabbed Ice King and shrieked in his ear,
"You lumping fool," she said. "We're not really here!"

There was a ringing, then, like a Christmas song.
And suddenly—*poof*—LSP was gone!
Ice King was back in his cold castle home.
But the old wizard sensed that he was not really alone . . .

Coming toward Ice King was a phantom, floating close.
Ice King howled, "Oh, come on, *no more ghosts*!"
Ice King pulled his bedsheets tight like a shield.
And then, through the darkness, two ghouls were revealed . . .

"It's us, Finn and Jake, *the Ghosts of Christmas Future!*"
And then—SMACK!—Jake punched Ice King in his icy-cold tooter.

We're showing you junk, Ice King. C'mon.
You're gonna peep the world after you're gone . . .

Everything changed, and they saw what was to come.
Ice King felt cold terror, from his head to his bum.
The Ice Castle towered over them, cracks all up the side.
Ice King realized, "So this is my home after I've died . . ."

Gunters marched from the castle, stretching for miles.
And each single Gunter was wearing a smile.

Do you know why they're so happy, waddling along?

They're happy, Ice King, because you are gone.

Next, they visited BMO, who was growing more sick.
Ice King cried, "Tell me this is just some cruel trick!"
But, no, it was true—BMO's flu had grown worse.
The tiny robot needed help—a doctor, a nurse!

But Ice King could do nothing but feel super sad
about the awful future that was to be had.

They visited the many princesses of Ooo.
All of them filled with delight anew.
Princesses dancing, happy and laughing.
The Ice King is gone—no more kidnapping!

NO MORE

Ice King did his best to hold back a tear.
"Now that I'm gone, they celebrate and cheer?"

At last they came to a grave, neglected and forgotten.
The headstone read, "Here lies a man who was really rotten."

Ice King cried, "No! I won't die a lonely wizard,
and go to my grave with a heart like a blizzard!
I understand now, this was some sort of test!
Am I stuck with this future? Please don't say yes!"

HERE LIES A
MAN WHO
WAS REALLY
ROTTEN

ICE
KING

But Finn and Jake were silent as they faded
into the mist.
Ice King howled, "I can change. I *will* change.
Please, I promise!"

And then Ice King was home, again in his bed,
warmth in the air from a sunrise all red.
He leaped to his feet, full of Christmas joy,
a feeling he hadn't felt since he was a young boy.

But Ice King was afraid. Was it too late?
How long had he been with those strange ghosts of fate?

Ice King ran to the window and looked out on the land.
"You hear that, Gunters? I am a changed man!"

"Now, Gunter, please tell me, what day is today?"
And one Gunter *wenked* in that penguin-y way.
"What's that you tell me? Christmas is not done?
Then look out, Ooo, 'cause *HERE I COME!*"

Ice King flew out into the morning and over the snow.
"First stop, the Tree Fort, to save tiny BMO!"

Ice King entered the fort and found the little dude,
curled up and sweating with robot flu.
"BMO, my friend, it seems you're dreadfully sick.
Let's see if a little *ice blast does the trick*!"

Ice King hit BMO with an icy-cold cure,
and—*snap!*—like that, BMO's flu was no more.

Then Ice King flew across Ooo, searching for friends,
hoping that he might make some amends.
He apologized to the princesses he'd harassed and annoyed.
"I know, now," he said, "life is to be enjoyed!"

But sadly for Ice King, the princesses didn't believe.
They said, "C'mon, Ice King, please just leave!"
So Ice King replied, "A Christmas party, tonight!
I'll prove to you all that I've seen the light!"

Ice King's Christmas celebration was a wonderful sight.
Everything was perfect and everything was right.

Jake said, "Yo, Ice King's not *totally* terrible."
LSP agreed, "It's a lumping Christmas miracle!"
Finn replied, "Y'know, maybe it's true . . ."
And BMO chimed in, "He did cure my flu!"

At last, Ice King spoke to his guests gathered from Ooo.
"Friends, I know you doubt that my change here is true.
But I promise you now, I *know* it will last!
I'm changed forever! The past is the past!
Those horrible ghouls that filled me with fear
have shown me the meaning of true Christmas cheer . . ."

"So please, oh please, heed my words as true,
or who knows what freaky ghosts might come and visit you.
Oh wait, just one more thing and then I'm done . . .
A happy Christmas to you and . . .

...glob bless us, everyone."